DC SUPER HEROES

SUPERGIRL™

AND THE
MAN OF METAL

WRITTEN BY
LAURIE S. SUTTON

ILLUSTRATED BY
GREGG SCHIGIEL

SUPERGIRL BASED ON CHARACTERS
CREATED BY JERRY SIEGEL AND JOE SHUSTER
BY SPECIAL ARRANGEMENT WITH THE JERRY SIEGEL FAMILY

STONE ARCH BOOKS
a capstone imprint

Published by Stone Arch Books, an imprint of Capstone.
1710 Roe Crest Drive
North Mankato, Minnesota 56003
www.capstonepub.com

Library of Congress Cataloging-in-Publication Data
Names: Sutton, Laurie S., author. | Schigiel, Gregg, illustrator.
Title: Supergirl and the man of metal / by Laurie S. Sutton ; illustrated by Gregg Schigiel.
Description: North Mankato, Minnesota : Stone Arch Books, an imprint of Capstone [2021] | Series: DC super hero adventures | Audience: Ages 8-11. | Audience: Grades 4-6. | Summary: Can the Girl of Steel keep a dangerous shipment of Kryptonite out of the clutches of the superpowered cyborg Metallo and save Metropolis from destruction at the same time?
Identifiers: LCCN 2020027234 (print) | LCCN 2020027235 (ebook) | ISBN 9781515882152 (library binding) | ISBN 9781515883241 (paperback) | ISBN 9781515892304 (pdf)
Subjects: CYAC: Superheroes—Fiction. | Supervillains—Fiction.
Classification: LCC PZ7.S968294 Su 2021 (print) | LCC PZ7.S968294 (ebook) | DDC [Fic]—dc23
LC record available at https://lccn.loc.gov/2020027234
LC ebook record available at https://lccn.loc.gov/2020027235

Designer: Hilary Wacholz

Printed in the United States   4869

TABLE OF CONTENTS

For nearly thirty years, Kal-El—better known as Superman—thought he was the sole survivor of the doomed planet Krypton. That changed when a second rocket ship crash-landed on Earth. Inside was Superman's teenage cousin, Kara Zor-El. She, too, had been sent from Krypton, but her ship was damaged in flight. Kara was put into a deep sleep that stopped her from aging. Soon after she arrived on Earth, Kara learned that she shared her cousin's extraordinary abilities fueled by the planet's yellow sun. She also found a new home with Jeremiah and Eliza Danvers. Now known to most as Kara Danvers, the teenager vowed to use her powers to protect Earth, just like her super hero cousin.

She became . . .

SUPERGIRL ™

CHAPTER 1

Turn Up the Heat

WHOOSH!

Supergirl flew above the streets of Metropolis. It was a bright morning and her shadow fell on the S.T.A.R. Labs armored truck below. The weekend traffic was not as crowded as it was during the workdays. That was a part of the plan to keep people safe. Just in case something went wrong. The truck needed a special super-hero guard because of what it was carrying—Kryptonite!

Kryptonite was a deadly substance to Supergirl and Superman. It was created when their home planet, Krypton, exploded. Pieces of the planet turned into radioactive meteoroids that spread out through space. Some of them landed on Earth as meteorites. Enemies of Supergirl and Superman were always looking for Kryptonite to use against the two heroes.

The S.T.A.R. Labs truck was taking a small sample of Kryptonite to one of their labs to experiment with it. Their scientists wanted to find a way to use it as a power source to help people.

To protect Supergirl, the Kryptonite sample had been locked in a lead container for this journey. Lead blocked the material's harmful radiation.

THWUUUMP!

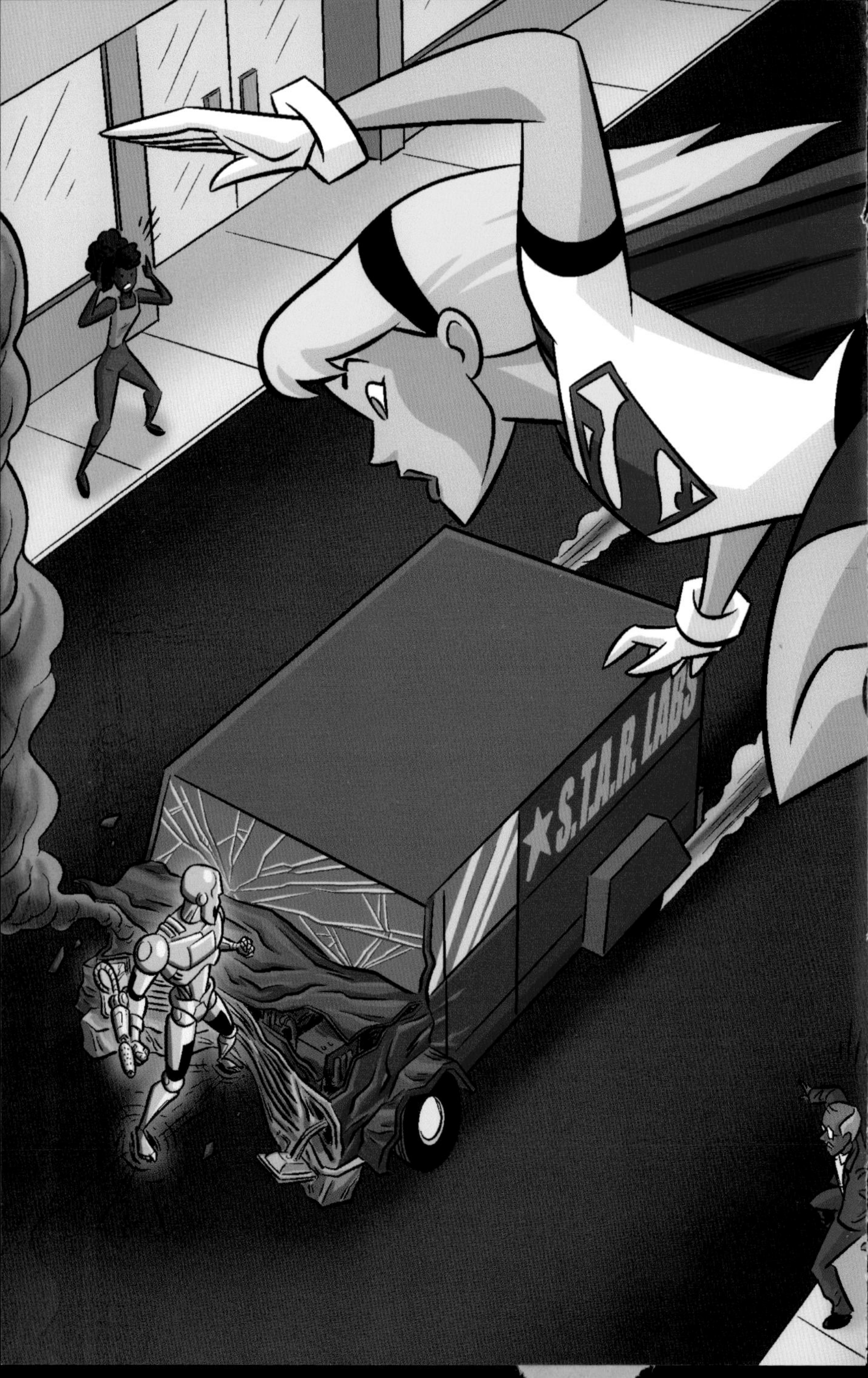
S.T.A.R. LABS

Suddenly something dropped down from the roof of a building. It was a robot in the shape of a man. He landed in front of the armored truck.

"Oh no! I can't stop in time!" the truck driver yelled.

Even with her super-speed, Supergirl could not halt the truck before it hit the robot.

CRAAASH!

Supergirl landed and helped the driver out of the wrecked vehicle. She made sure he was not injured before she turned toward the robot. But she already knew it was more than a robot. She recognized the super-villain.

"Metallo!" Supergirl said.

"In the flesh, as they say," Metallo replied. "Except that my body is made of a special alloy and I haven't been human in years."

The Girl of Steel looked at his mechanical form. He was a man of metal from head to toe. She guessed that he wanted the Kryptonite sample in the armored truck.

Metallo used Kryptonite as his power source. Right now a chunk of Kryptonite sat inside a compartment in his metal chest. It was not safe for Supergirl to get too close to him.

"I see you've added something new," Supergirl said, pointing at a high-tech laser mounted on his right forearm.

"Yes. Let me show you how it works," Metallo said.

ZIIIISSSSS! A ray of intense green energy shot out from the device and hit Supergirl. She was surprised when she actually felt pain! The bright-green beam started to burn the S-shield on her costume.

HA! HA! HA! Metallo laughed. "How do you like my special laser beam? You can feel it because it uses radiation from my Kryptonite power source."

"Uhhh. Yes, I can feel it," Supergirl said, gritting her teeth against the pain. "But thanks for explaining it to me. Now I know what I'm up against."

Supergirl zoomed forward and delivered a super-punch that knocked Metallo down the city block.

POWWW! SMAAASH!

Metallo landed on top of a parked car. It was flattened, but the super-villain rolled off the wreck as if he was rolling out of bed.

"My body is just as tough as yours, Supergirl," Metallo boasted. "You can't hurt me no matter how hard you try."

ZIIIISSSSS!

The villain used his Kryptonite energy laser to set the crushed car on fire. Then he picked the car up and threw it at Supergirl at the other end of the city block.

FWOOOOSH!

Supergirl used her super-breath to blow out the flames like a birthday candle before the vehicle reached her. She caught the burned car easily and held it above her head.

"Let's test how tough you are, Metallo," Supergirl said.

Supergirl crushed the car into a compact ball and threw it at Metallo like a baseball pitcher aiming for a strike. The villain managed to catch it, but the force of the hero's throw pushed him even farther down the street.

"Hey! That's my car!" a man yelled. He came out of a nearby donut shop and pushed his way through a small crowd of people. They had gathered to watch the battle between the Girl of Steel and the man of metal.

"Okay, you can have it back," Metallo said. The super-villain tossed the car at the man—and the crowd.

"No!" Supergirl shouted. She used her super-speed to race to the rescue.

WOOOOSH!

Supergirl moved so fast that she was a blur of red and blue.

That will keep her busy while I get what I came for, Metallo thought. He made a powerful leap and landed next to the armored truck.

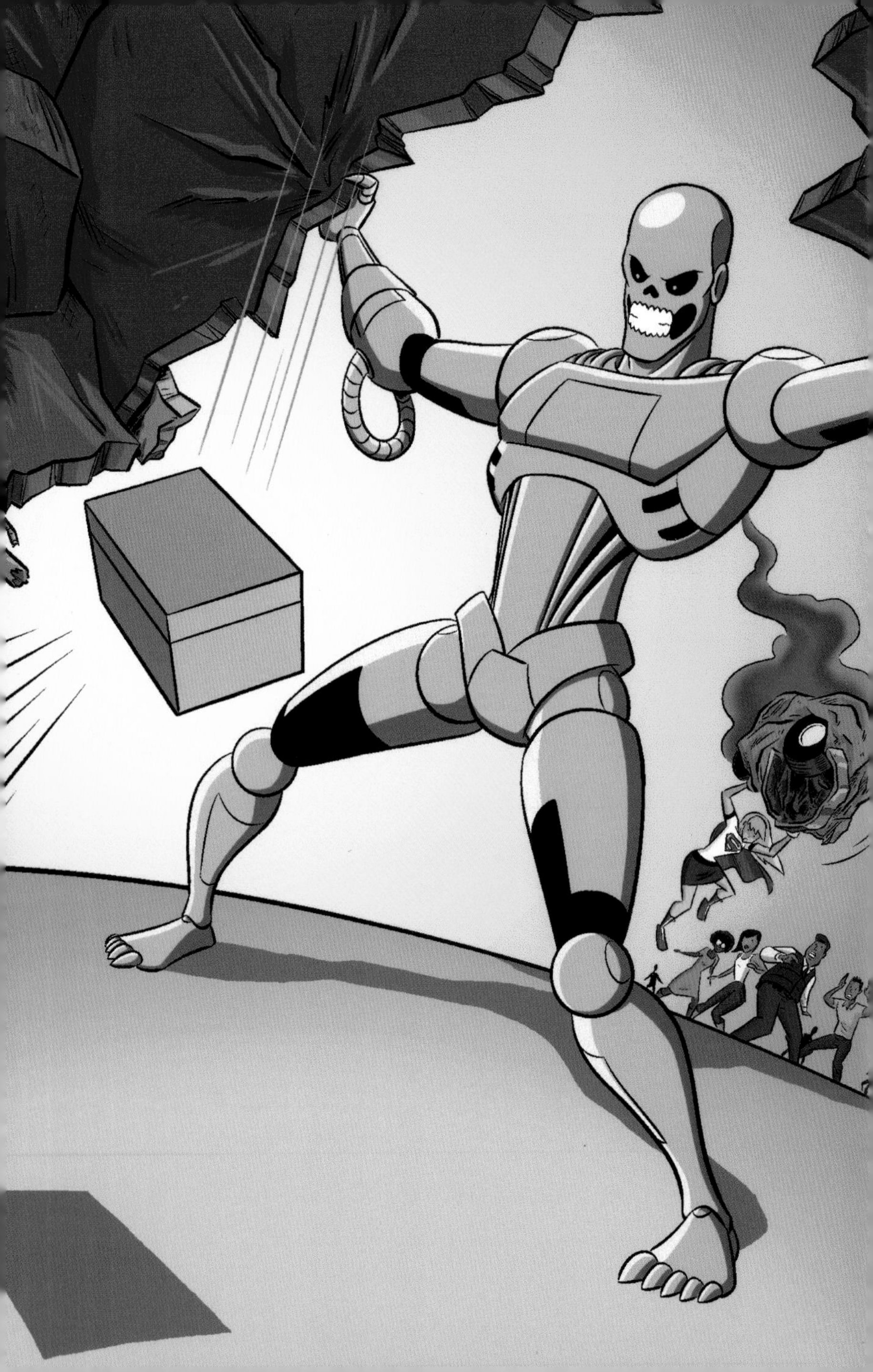

The villain picked up the vehicle as if it were a toy and ripped it open. A single lead box fell out. It was the size of a lunch box.

It's smaller than I thought, but it's what's inside that matters, Metallo decided. He dropped the armored truck and reached for the small container holding the Kryptonite.

Down at the other end of the block, Supergirl had caught the car and saved the bystanders. She turned in time to see Metallo reach for the little lead box.

I have to stop him from getting his hands on the Kryptonite, Supergirl thought. *And he has actually given me an idea how to do that.*

Just as Metallo had ripped the armored truck in half, Supergirl did the same thing to the wrecked car. She gripped the two pieces in each hand and flew toward the villain at top speed.

SMAAAASH!

Supergirl slammed the halves against Metallo. It happened so fast that the villain was taken by surprise. He did not have time to grab the box of Kryptonite.

SIZZZZZLE!

Supergirl used her heat vision to melt the car around the super-villain. She molded it with her hands until it was a smooth sphere. Metallo was trapped inside.

People gathered to cheer Supergirl and her victory.

"Yay, Supergirl!"

"Way to go!"

"That took care of him!"

Supergirl put the big metal ball down on the ground.

"Sorry about your car," Supergirl said to the owner.

"My family is never going to believe what happened," the fellow said as he shook his head.

Supergirl floated over to where the lead box rested on the street. She was about to pick it up when she heard a strange sound.

ZIIIISSSSS!

It was coming from inside the metal ball. A few seconds later, a beam of bright-green light came out of the ball. The beam started to slice through the metal.

Metallo is using his Kryptonite laser to escape, Supergirl realized.

CHAPTER 2

Sky Fight

ZIIIISSSSS!

The metal ball was cut apart in moments. Metallo burst out of his prison. The crowd ran for safe shelter. Supergirl stood her ground and faced the villain.

The lead box lay on the ground between them.

"You can't stop me from getting what I came for, Supergirl," Metallo said.

The villain opened the compartment in his robot chest. It revealed his power source—a chunk of glowing, green Kryptonite. Supergirl instantly felt its harmful rays wash over her, even stronger than the laser.

"Ohhh," Supergirl moaned. The strength drained from her body, and she fell to one knee.

Metallo stood over the hero and pointed the laser at her.

"Because of this metal body, I have no sense of taste or touch or smell," Metallo said. "But I can feel a sense of satisfaction when I destroy you."

ZIIIISSS! Metallo fired the Kryptonite laser at Supergirl. Once again its beam hit the S-shield on her chest and burned her costume. Even the super-strong fabric was affected by the Kryptonite, just as she was.

I have to get out of range before I get too weak, Supergirl thought. *But I have to make sure Metallo doesn't get his hands on that box of Kryptonite.*

WOOOOSH!

Supergirl used what was left of her super-speed to grab the little lead container. Then she leaped into the air and flew into the bright-blue sky.

"Nooo!" Metallo shouted.

The super-villain could not fly, but his mechanical body gave him enormous strength. He used it to leap after his foe.

As soon as Supergirl got far enough from Metallo, her strength returned. She paused in midair and searched for the villain with her super-vision. No matter what, she did not want him to escape.

I can't get close enough to Metallo to fight him hand-to-hand, Supergirl thought. *I'll have to find another way to defeat him. But first, I have to find him.*

It turned out that Metallo was not hard to locate. Supergirl spotted him leaping toward her from the roof of a tall building.

ZIIIISSS!

Metallo fired the Kryptonite energy beam at the Girl of Steel. She dodged out of the way, but the beam sliced through a cell phone tower on the roof of a nearby building. The tower started to topple and fall.

"You have terrible aim," Supergirl said as she zoomed to catch the tumbling tower.

Metallo landed on the top of another building and used it like a stepping-stone to leap at Supergirl again.

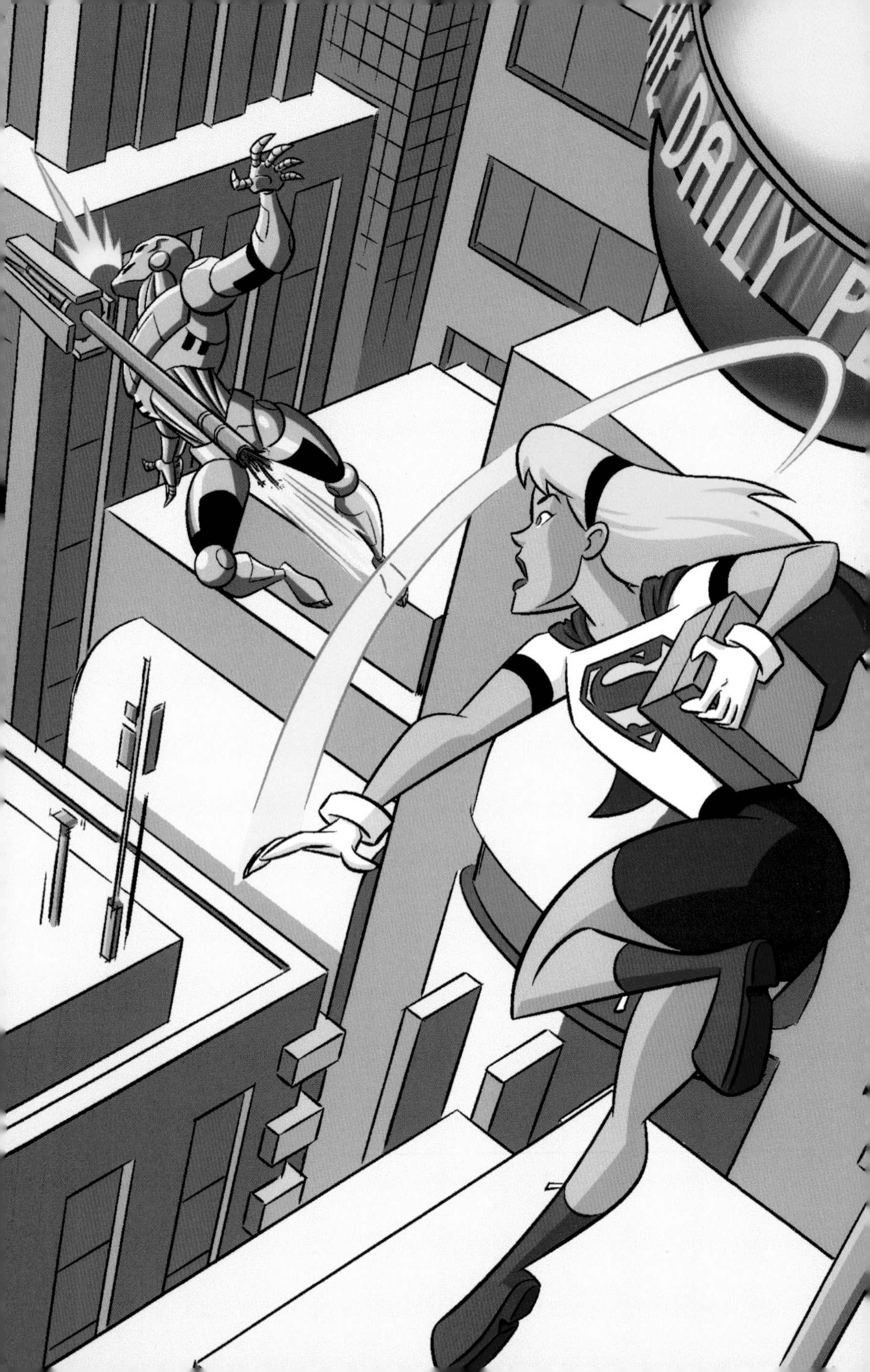
DAILY

"On the other hand," Supergirl said, "my aim is super-accurate."

The Girl of Steel threw the metal tower straight toward the villain and knocked him out of the sky.

THWUUUMP!

Metallo crashed into the street below. The pavement was cracked and damaged, but the man of metal was not. A moment later he was back on his feet.

"It will take more than that to stop me," Metallo said. The villain leaped back into the air toward Supergirl.

WOOOOSH!

It was easy for Supergirl to zip out of the way and avoid Metallo.

WOOOSH! WHOOOSH!

The hero kept him jumping from place to place, always missing his target. But Supergirl was buying time until she found a way to stop Metallo. She needed to knock him out, and to do that she needed to hit him with something bigger than a car or metal cell tower.

"Ah! Found it!" Supergirl said as she spotted a nearby construction site.

WHOOSH!

Still holding the lead box in one hand, Supergirl zoomed down to the worksite. As Metallo dropped out of the sky toward her, Supergirl picked up a huge dump truck with her free hand. With a flick of her wrist, she threw it at the villain.

WHAAAAM! Metallo could not move out of the way. The truck hit him in midair and knocked him to the ground.

THUUUUD!

The impact made a large crater in the middle of the street like a meteorite strike.

Supergirl flew over to the spot to find out if Metallo had been knocked out at last. She didn't see any movement.

"I guess Metallo isn't that tough after all," Supergirl said.

The hero lifted the dump truck off Metallo with one hand, but he wasn't there.

"Where did he go?" Supergirl gasped.

BOOM! Suddenly the villain burst up out of the ground behind her.

ZIIIISSS!

Metallo fired a Kryptonite laser blast that hit her in the back. Supergirl stumbled and fell to her knees.

"Surprise," Metallo said. "I tunneled out from under the dump truck. I'm not that easy to beat."

The villain opened the compartment in his robot chest and added the rays of his Kryptonite power source to his attack on Supergirl.

"I told you that my body is made of a special alloy," Metallo said. "You can hit me with a megaton bomb and it wouldn't hurt me. A dump truck is nothing."

Supergirl struggled to her feet and bravely turned to face Metallo. She held the little lead box in front of her like a shield. It wasn't much of a defense against the villain's powerful energy ray. The box began to melt.

"That box won't protect you," Metallo said. "Hand it over or I'll take it from you."

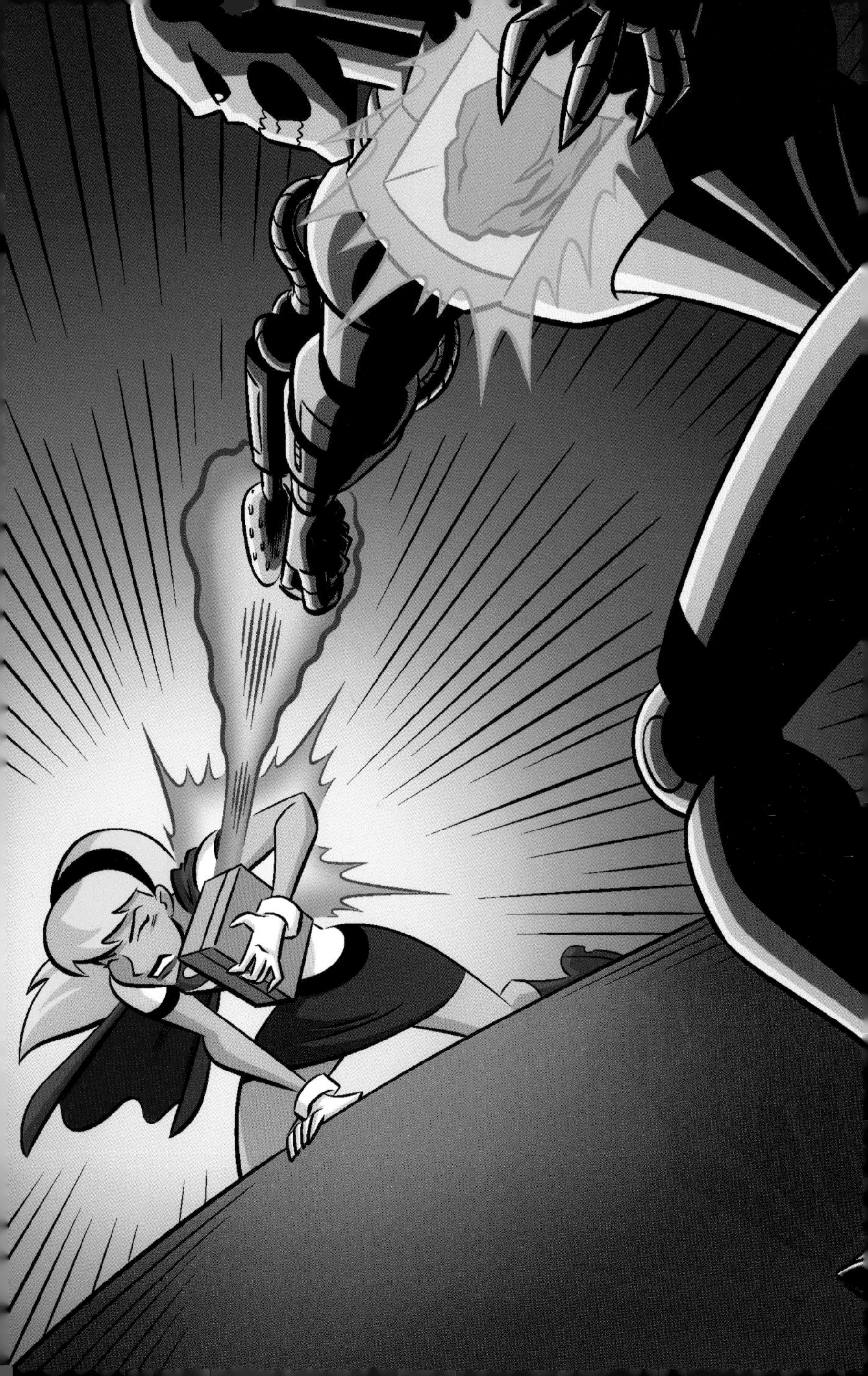

The lead box softened in Supergirl's hands. As her fingers sank into its sides, she got an idea.

"Okay, fine. Since you want this box so badly," the Girl of Steel said suddenly, "you can have it."

SIZZZZ!

Supergirl used her heat vision to melt the lead container. The metal still covered the Kryptonite inside, so Supergirl was safe from its radiation. But then she shoved the molten blob into Metallo's chest compartment.

FWOOOOSH!

A quick blast of freezing super-breath hardened the blob. It was instantly fused to Metallo's chest. The lead blocked the rays of the villain's Kryptonite power source.

"Nooo!" Metallo yelled.

SCRAPE! SCRAPE!

The super-villain stopped shooting his Kryptonite laser and clawed at the lead blob on his chest. He knew that he had just lost his most powerful weapon against Supergirl. The Kryptonite laser beam was not as strong as the chunk of Kryptonite in his chest.

For the first time during their battle, Metallo actually looked worried.

CHAPTER 3

Destruction Zone

Supergirl knew that she could not let Metallo uncover the Kryptonite in his chest compartment. She had to keep him busy until she could find a way to disable his power source and shut him down.

Supergirl grabbed the villain by the arm laser and used it to swing him around and around above her head. She spun him faster and faster until he was a blur.

"Let's see if your mechanical body can get dizzy," Supergirl said.

"Ooof," Metallo moaned.

Supergirl saw that another crowd was gathering to watch the battle.

I have to move this fight away from all these people, Supergirl thought. *That construction site is a good place. It's the weekend and there aren't any workers there.*

SIZZZZ!

Supergirl used her heat vision to slice Metallo's arm laser away from his forearm. It wasn't made from the same metal as his body. She held on to the device and the villain sailed off into the air. Supergirl crushed the Kryptonite laser into scrap metal as she flew after Metallo.

SMAAAASH!

Metallo landed right where Supergirl had aimed—in the boom of a construction crane. As Metallo struggled to untangle himself, the hero swooped down and twisted it around the villain like a rope.

"This won't hold me!" Metallo boasted.

"It doesn't have to—for long," Supergirl replied.

The Girl of Steel flew over to where two cement trucks were parked. She lifted one in each hand and floated through the air. She hovered above Metallo.

Just as he had promised, the super-villain broke free from the boom twisted around his body. He looked up at his foe.

"Hitting me with a truck didn't work the last time," Metallo said. "Hitting me with two more won't be any better."

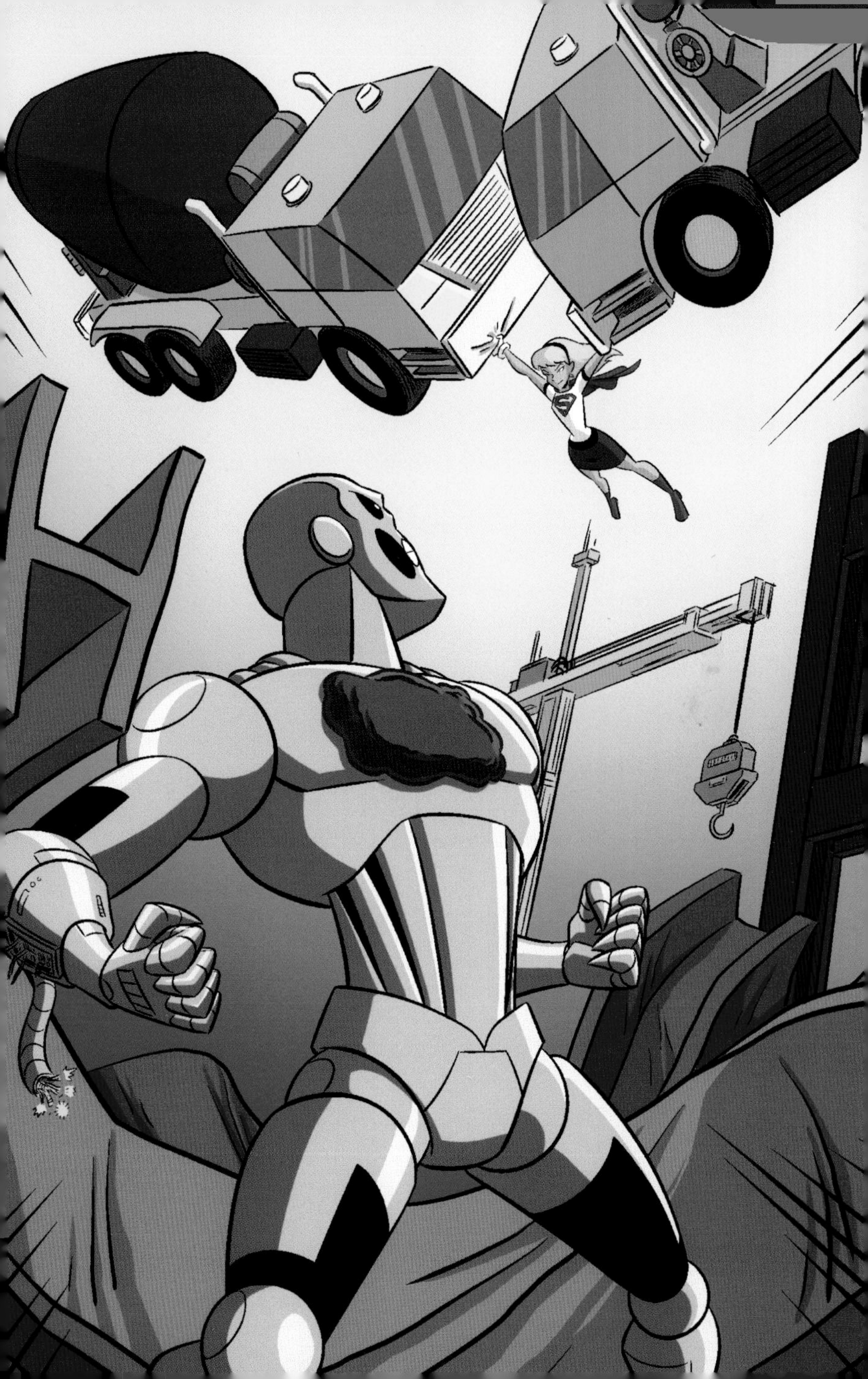

"Don't worry, I'm not going to hit you," Supergirl said.

CRAAAAK!

The hero smashed the two trucks together. They cracked like eggs and gushed cement. **SPLOOSH!** It spilled all over Metallo until he was completely covered.

FWOOOSH!

Supergirl used her super-breath to dry the cement until it hardened. Soon Metallo was surrounded by a giant block of solid concrete.

He doesn't have his laser to slice him out this time, Supergirl thought.

RUUUUMBLE!

Suddenly the concrete block shook. Cracks formed on its sides. They grew larger and wider until the block burst apart and the super-villain was free.

"Nice try, Supergirl," Metallo said, "but it's going to take more than that to stop me."

"You keep saying that," Supergirl replied.

The villain picked up a huge chunk of the broken concrete and threw it at Supergirl. She could not avoid being hit, and the force of the blow knocked her backward.

THWUUUMP! She hit one of the support columns of the building under construction. The impact made the building shudder.

"Is that all you've got?" Supergirl asked as she got to her feet. She tossed aside the chunk of concrete like a pebble. "You're not so tough without your laser and the Kryptonite in your chest."

If the villain's mechanical face had been able to show emotion, it would have revealed his fury. A power surge made his eyes flash.

"I don't need them to destroy you," Metallo growled. "I can do it with my bare hands."

The man of metal launched himself at the Girl of Steel. He slammed into her like a missile. Metallo drove his foe into several steel support columns, one after another.

THWUUMP! THWUUMP! THWUUMP!

The columns broke off and stacked up like pancakes against Supergirl's back. The building shifted and groaned. The columns helped hold up the structure, and without them it was ready to collapse.

Metallo shoved Supergirl all the way through the building and out the other side. He was about to ram her into a concrete wall, but Supergirl planted her feet on the ground and used her super-strength to stop. She pushed the villain away from her.

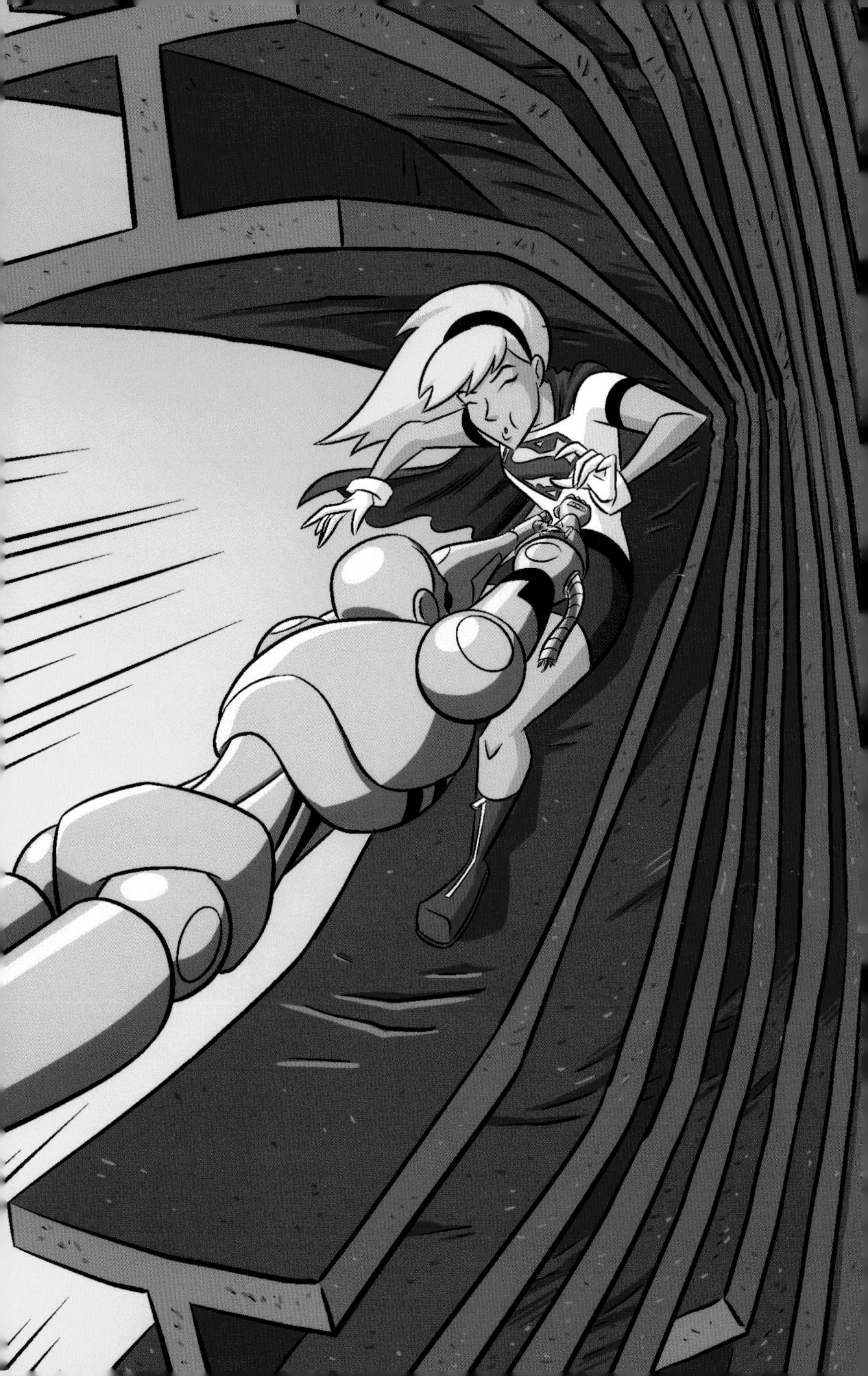

"You think your special alloy makes you indestructible," Supergirl said. "We'll see about that."

Supergirl fired twin beams of heat vision at the super-villain. They hit his arms and legs like a laser. The alloy that made up his mechanical body glowed where the superpowered heat hit it, but it did not melt.

"Ha! Ha! Ha! Your heat vision doesn't even make a scratch," Metallo laughed.

FWOOOSH!

Suddenly Supergirl switched to her freezing super-breath. Instantly the villain's alloy got super-cold. His joints froze. He could not move. Then all the moisture in the air around Metallo froze and formed a block of ice around him. But, just as with the block of concrete, it wasn't long before Metallo used his super-strength to burst out of his prison.

Supergirl quickly used her heat vision to heat up Metallo's entire body. Then she used her freezing super-breath to make him super-cold. She switched back and forth between the two extremes. Hot, cold. Hot, cold. Hot, cold.

The quick changes in temperature should stress even Metallo's special alloy and make it break, Supergirl thought. *I hope.*

The hero was surprised that Metallo just stood there and did not try to stop her from what she was doing.

Has his brain been affected by the extreme changes in temperature? Supergirl wondered. *That's the only part of him that isn't made of metal. Maybe I knocked him out and he just hasn't fallen over.*

Supergirl stopped attacking the villain with her heat vision and super-breath.

"Finally!" Metallo said. "I was getting tired of you doing whatever it was you were doing."

The man of metal rushed toward Supergirl, ready to fight her hand-to-hand. He was strong, but he was not as fast as the Girl of Steel. She used her super-speed to step out of the way. As he passed, Supergirl grabbed him by the arm and threw him toward the damaged building.

SMAAASH! SMAAASH! SMAAAASH!

Metallo crashed into the last few support columns that were holding up the structure. Before the villain knew what was happening, the building collapsed on top of him.

BWOOOOM!

Supergirl put her hands on her hips and looked at the tremendous pile of rubble.

"Well, it's not a megaton bomb, but that should be enough to finally knock out Metallo," Supergirl said.

RUUUMBLE!

Chunks of concrete and twisted steel beams shifted as if something were digging up from below. Supergirl groaned. She could guess who it was.

"Metallo!" Supergirl said.

CHAPTER 4

Escape Plan

The super-villain crawled up out of the tons of broken concrete. He moved slowly and looked as if he was tired. This time he did not make a snappy comment to Supergirl about being unstoppable.

Well, that looks like it at least slowed him down, Supergirl thought.

Metallo rose to his feet on the top of the debris pile. He looked down at Supergirl. She stood ready to continue their battle.

Although Metallo would never admit defeat, he was tired of fighting the Girl of Steel. She matched him in strength and stamina. They could go on like this for a very long time. Now, he didn't want to. It had been fun to taunt her at the beginning of their battle, but now it wasn't. It was time for him to leave.

"I have the Kryptonite I came for," Metallo declared. "Even though it's sealed inside my chest compartment, I'll find a way to get at it. This isn't over, Supergirl. Mark my words!"

Metallo leaped into the air, away from the construction site. It took the hero a moment to realize he was escaping.

"He's not going to get away from me that easily," Supergirl said as she took off after the super-villain.

Metallo leaped from building to building as fast as his mechanical legs could carry him. And everywhere he went he left a trail of destruction behind him.

This will slow her down, Metallo thought as he threw a huge air-conditioning unit off the roof of one building.

Supergirl zoomed down at super-speed to save people on the street from the falling unit. Metallo leaped to the top floor of a city parking lot and tossed several vehicles high into the air.

"Catch, Supergirl!" Metallo shouted.

WHOOOSH! WHOOOSH!

The Girl of Steel flew at super-speed and caught two of the cars easily. But now her hands were full. A third vehicle plunged toward people sitting at an outdoor café.

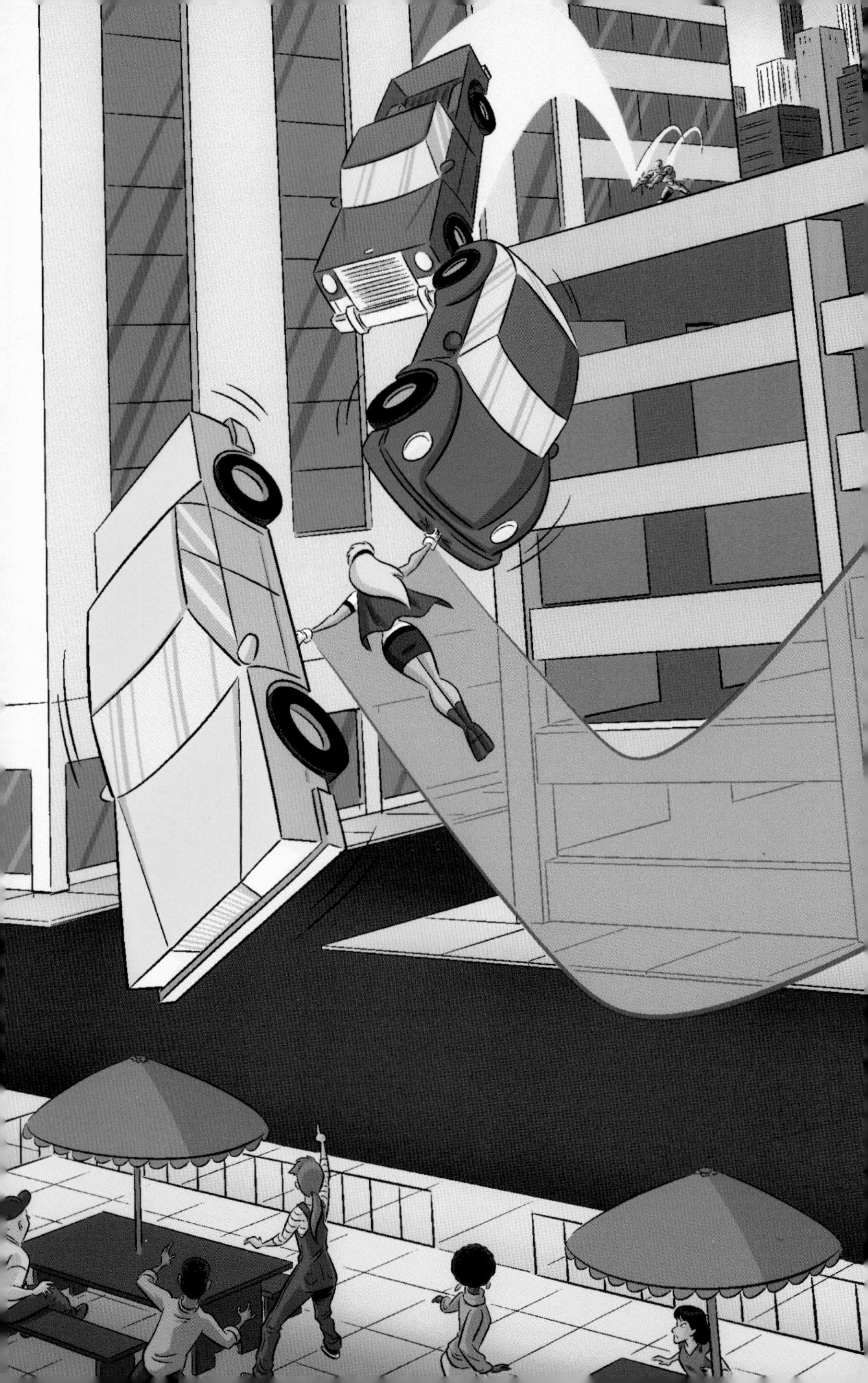

FWOOOOSH!

Supergirl used her super-breath to blow the truck away from the people. Then she used her breath to make a cushion of air beneath the truck and gently lower it to the ground. The Girl of Steel landed next to it and put down the two cars she held. The customers at the café clapped and cheered.

Metallo is trying to keep me busy so he can escape, Supergirl thought. *He's putting people in danger. He has to be stopped.*

Supergirl flew back into the air. She spotted Metallo leaping toward the Metropolis Bridge. The suspension bridge spanned Metropolis Bay and was full of traffic.

"Oh no," Supergirl said. She could guess what the villain was about to do.

Just as Supergirl feared, Metallo landed on the bridge in the middle of the road.

HONNNK! HONNNK!

Cars and trucks swerved to avoid hitting the man of metal. Metallo paid no attention to the confusion he was causing as he walked over to where the suspension cables were attached to the side of the bridge. They held up the roadway loaded with traffic. Metallo grabbed one of the thick cables in his powerful hands and pulled it apart.

SNAAAAP!

The cable broke in two. Metallo leaped over to another cable.

SNAAAAP!

The super-villain tore it in half.

SNAP! SNAP! SNAP!

Metallo went down one side of the bridge and destroyed as many of the suspension cables as possible before Supergirl could arrive. The roadway tipped dangerously to one side. Cars and trucks slid toward the edge of the bridge.

This will keep Supergirl busy long enough for me to make my getaway, Metallo thought.

Supergirl zoomed to the bridge at top speed. She grabbed the snapped ends of one of the middle cables and used her incredible strength to hold it together. Even her super-strong muscles felt the strain of holding up the weight of the roadway and all the cars and trucks on it.

"Uugghh!" Supergirl groaned.

But the roadway stopped tipping. The cars stopped sliding toward the edge of the bridge. Everyone was safe for the moment.

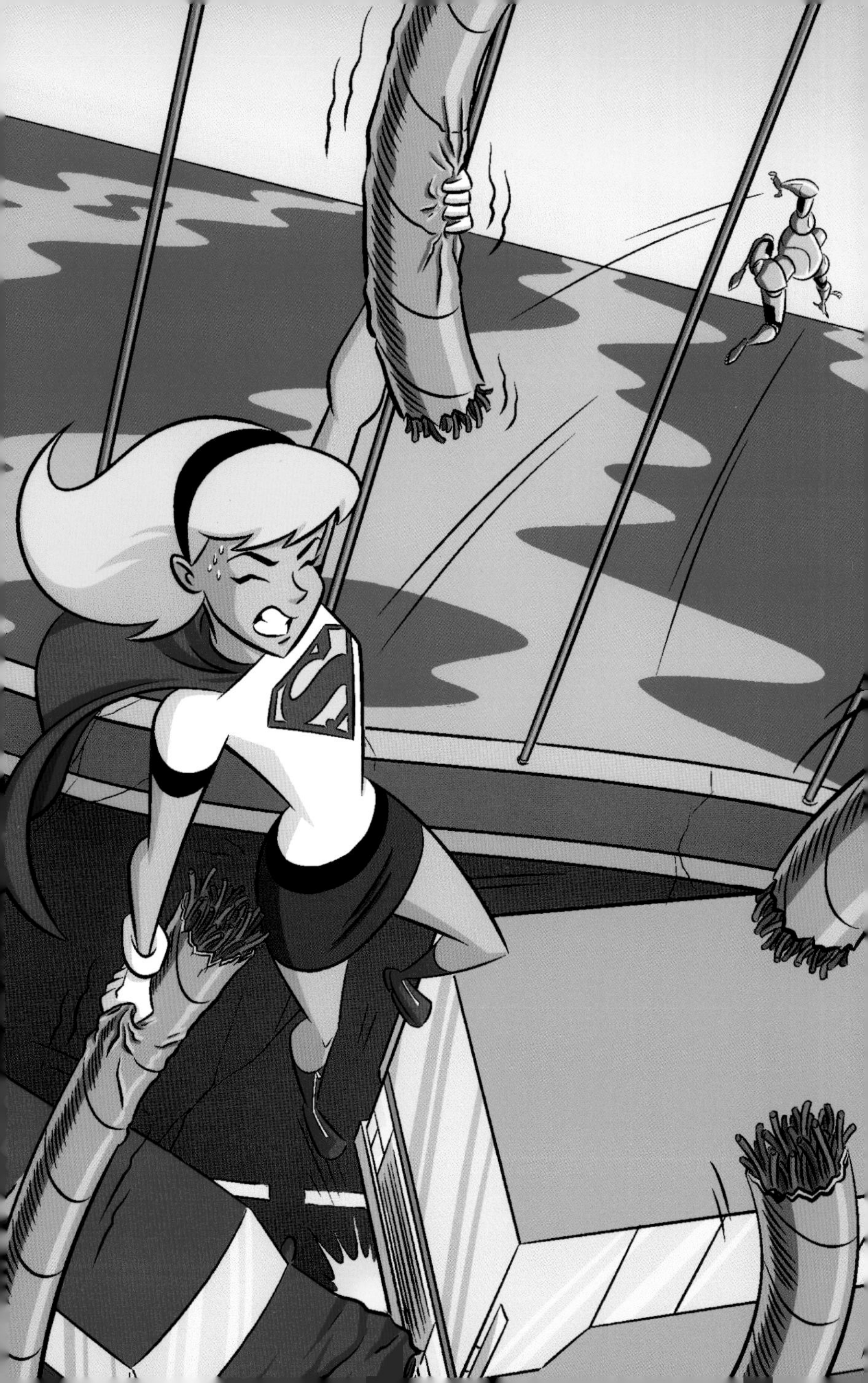

Metallo did a lot of damage, Supergirl thought. *And now it's up to me to fix it.*

SIZZZZ!

The hero used her heat vision to melt the two ends of the broken cable back together. Then she used her freezing super-breath to cool the molten metal and make the connection solid and strong.

Supergirl did the same thing to each of the suspension cables that Metallo had snapped. One after another, she repaired what the villain had wrecked. The bridge was safe again and the people unharmed. But Metallo had escaped.

He might have gotten away for now, but I'll find him, Supergirl thought. *I just need to get high enough to spot him.*

WHOOSH!

The Girl of Steel flew high into the sky. Soon she was far above the bridge and Metropolis Bay.

Supergirl stopped and hovered in midair. The whole city was spread out below her. She could see all the way to the horizon.

Metallo is out there somewhere, Supergirl thought as she used her super-vision to search for the villain.

Supergirl slowly turned around in a circle. She switched back and forth between her telescopic vision and her X-ray vision to look for Metallo. She used her telescopic vision to search everywhere outside, on the streets and rooftops, and in the parks of Metropolis. Then she used her X-ray vision to search inside the buildings, underground in the subway, and in every vehicle moving across the city.

Supergirl got a glimpse of everyone in Metropolis. She saw kids playing in the parks, people walking their pets, and crowds out shopping on the weekend. She saw police and firefighters working on the scene of the wrecked S.T.A.R. Labs armored truck and the sites of her battles with Metallo.

As Supergirl continued to turn, she looked inside the Daily Planet Building, where reporters sat at their desks, even on the weekend, writing their stories.

She scanned the basements and elevator shafts of every building that had them. She saw people in their homes and apartments watching television, cooking, doing laundry, and living their everyday lives.

But there was no sign of Metallo.

Be patient, Supergirl reminded herself. *You know he's out there somewhere.*

The Girl of Steel had almost turned around in a full circle when she finally spotted the villain. He was inside the huge hydroelectric power plant just outside the city limits. The plant generated electricity for Metropolis. She saw that he was putting together some sort of device.

I don't know what Metallo is building, but it can't be good, Supergirl thought.

BWOOOM!

The Girl of Steel took off at supersonic speed and headed for the power plant to stop Metallo.

CHAPTER 5

Power Play

The weekend-shift workers at the power plant were not surprised to see Supergirl. They had already seen Metallo stomp into the plant a few minutes ago.

"Supergirl, we're glad you're here! There's a robot man heading for the main powerhouse!" one of the workers said. "He looked dangerous."

"He is. Everyone should get out of the power plant," Supergirl told him.

She knew that her earlier battles with Metallo had caused major damage. She was sure it would happen here too. Supergirl did not want anyone to get hurt by accident.

Once she was sure that all the workers were gone, Supergirl flew deeper into the building to face Metallo. He was in the main powerhouse. It was a gigantic chamber with rows of enormous electric generators. Inside each generator, huge blades spun at top speed to create the electricity to power Metropolis.

Supergirl saw that Metallo had hooked up the motor of an industrial arc welder to the top of one of the hydroelectric generators. A tube and welding torch were connected to the motor. But Supergirl knew he wasn't going to use the torch to weld metal together. He was going to use it to cut metal.

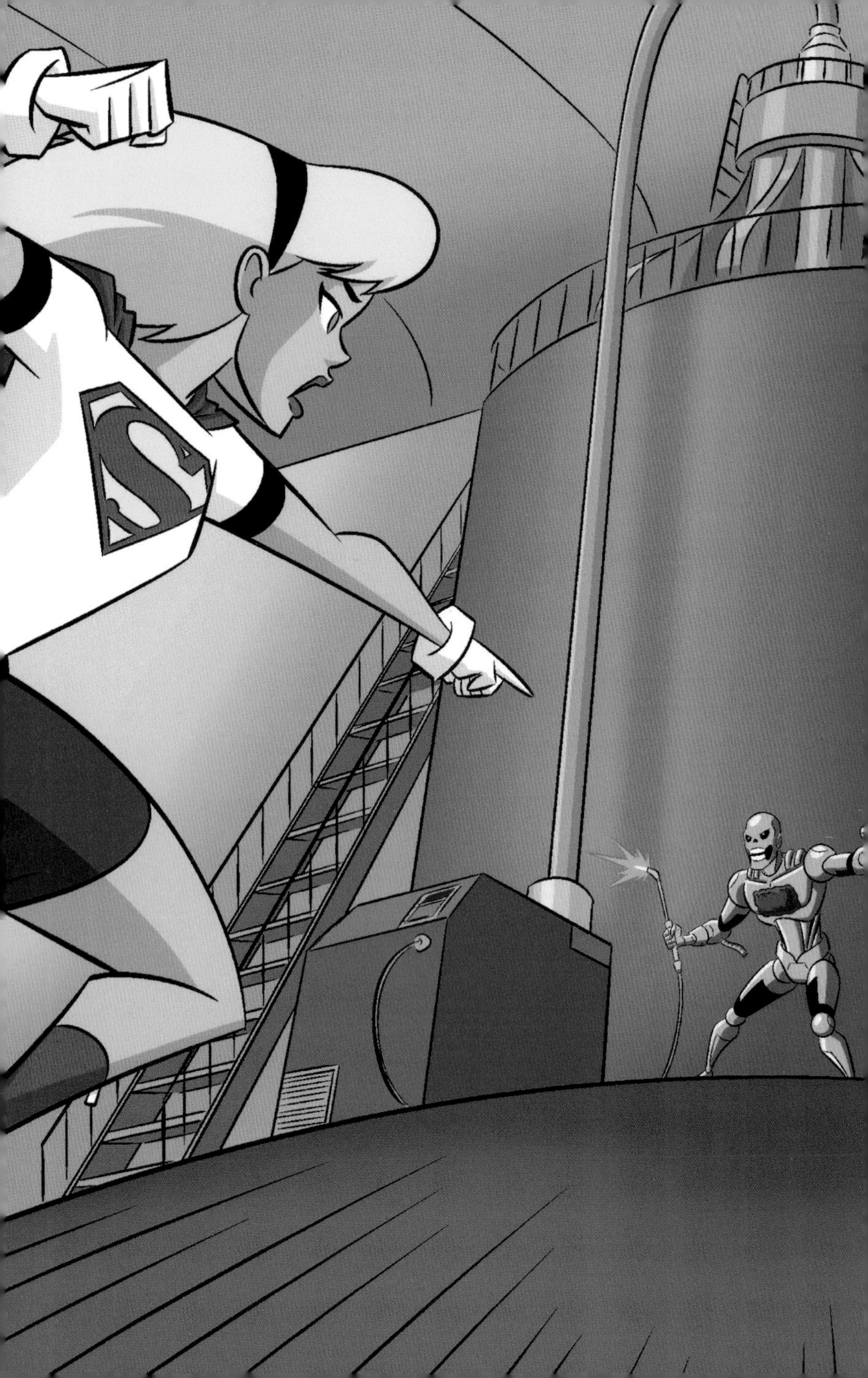

He plans to cut away the lead in his chest to get at the Kryptonite, Supergirl realized. *And he needs the power from the hydroelectric generator to boost the torch.*

"I know what you're up to," the hero said.

"What? Supergirl! How did you find me?" Metallo asked, startled. "Never mind. You can't stop me."

Metallo flipped a switch on the torch and a bright-blue flame shot out.

"You keep saying that." Supergirl sighed.

The hero zoomed toward the super-villain. She reached out and grabbed the torch in his hand. Supergirl tried to wrestle it out of Metallo's grip, but he was just as strong as she was. He would not let go of it.

Strength alone isn't going to work, Supergirl thought. *I have to try something else.*

Suddenly Supergirl kicked Metallo's legs out from under him. The villain shouted in surprise as he fell. But he did not let go of the cutting torch. Neither did Supergirl. She landed on top of him.

"Let's see if this amped-up torch can cut through your special alloy," Supergirl said as she pushed the flame toward Metallo's shoulder joint.

"Let's not," Metallo replied as he tried to push the flame away.

"You sound worried," Supergirl said.

Metallo *was* worried, but he could not let his foe know that. The super-villain twisted his mechanical body and broke free of Supergirl's grip. She lost her hold on the torch for a moment. Metallo used that split second to rush forward and throw the hero backward.

SMAAASH! Supergirl crashed into a wall.

Metallo quickly put the cutting torch up against the lead blob melted onto his chest. **SIIIIZ!** Sparks flew out when the flame hit the metal. A second later, the torch stopped working.

"What . . . what happened?" Metallo gasped. He stared at the torch.

"I pulled the plug," Supergirl said. She stood on top of the hydroelectric generator and held up the power cable that had connected the arc welder's motor to the generator.

"Nooo!" Metallo yelled. He was so angry that he picked up the heavy arc welder and threw it at the Girl of Steel.

"Temper, temper," Supergirl said as she easily caught the big welding machine.

Supergirl threw the machine back at Metallo. **_WHAAAM!_** It hit him and knocked him off his feet.

The super-villain was thrown backward. **_CRAAASH!_** He slammed up against the side of one of the hydroelectric generators.

Metallo staggered a few feet away from the massive generator, revealing a giant crack the impact had made in the outer wall. Suddenly the huge turbine blades were exposed. They spun like an enormous boat propeller going at high speed.

ZZZZT! CRAAAAKLE! ZZZZT!

Huge arcs of electricity leaped out of the crack in the damaged generator. They hit Metallo's metal body like lightning bolts. The villain gripped the sides of his head in pain.

"Ahhhh! My circuitry!" Metallo moaned. He fell to his knees.

That super-jolt of electricity disrupted his electronic systems, Supergirl realized. *That's the first sign of weakness I've seen in him. I can use it to defeat him!*

The Girl of Steel flew down from the top of the hydroelectric generator. Before Metallo could react, she grabbed him in a wrestling hold. She turned him around to face the crackling electricity coming out of the split in the generator.

Metallo knew he was in danger of defeat. He struggled against Supergirl's hold. But some of his circuits were damaged and he could not call up the full strength of his mechanical body.

"Let's end this right now," Supergirl said.

Still holding Metallo in a tight grip, the hero turned the villain around and pushed him toward the crack in the hydroelectric generator. The raging bolts of electricity stretched out toward Metallo.

CRAAAAKLE! BOOOM!

The blue bolts surrounded Supergirl and Metallo. A web of sizzling electricity wrapped around them. Supergirl was not harmed. But Metallo's metal body was a perfect conductor. His special alloy could not protect him from the high voltage. Electricity raced through every wire, chip, and circuit inside the villain and shorted him out. Metallo was knocked out at last. He went limp in Supergirl's grip.

WHIIIR! HUMMMM! CLUNK!

The damaged hydroelectric generator shut down. The bolts of wild electricity stopped. Supergirl lowered Metallo to the ground.

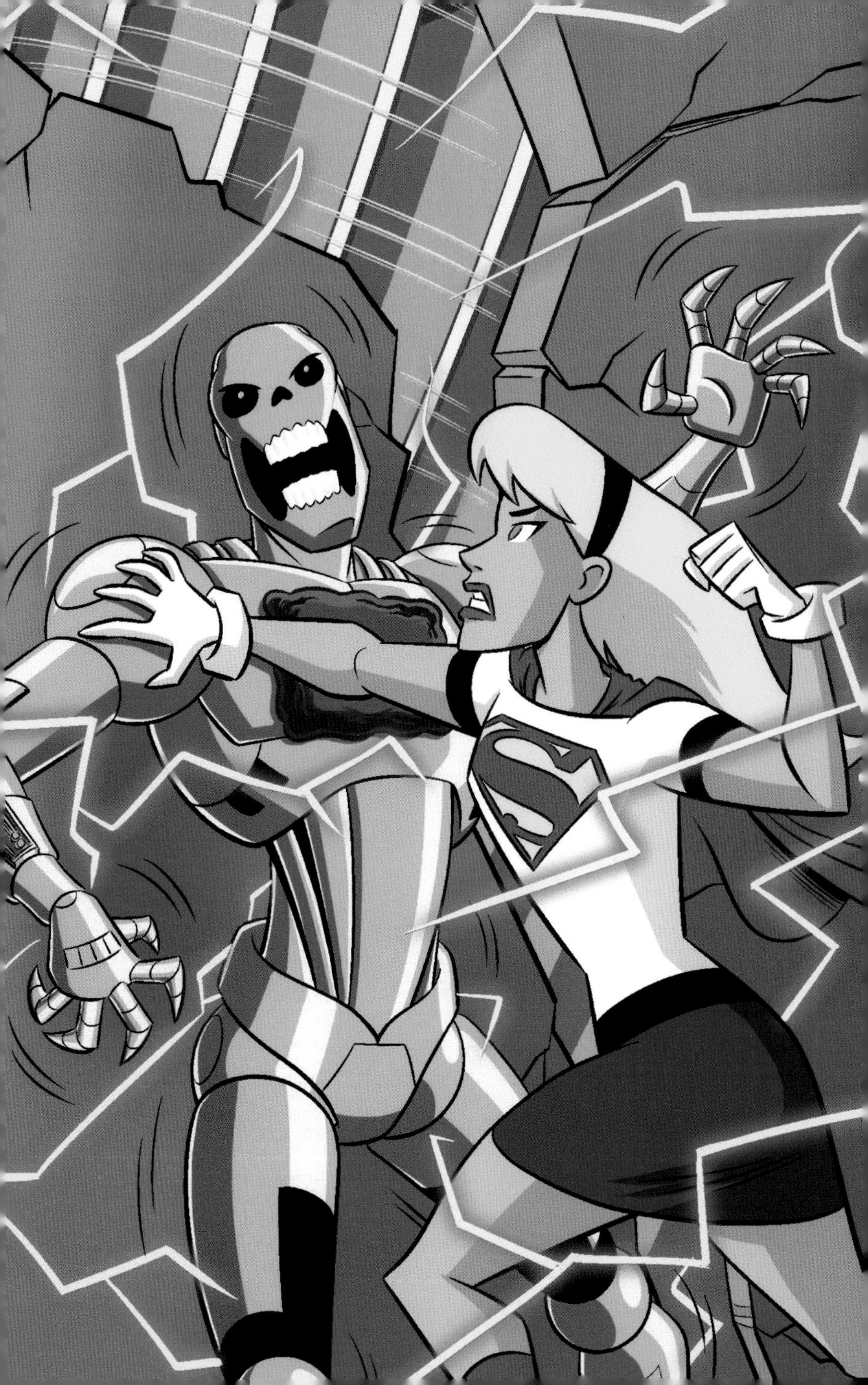

Metallo is knocked out for now, but for how long? Supergirl realized. *There's only one way to make sure he's shut down for good. I have to remove his power source.*

Supergirl used her heat vision to carefully slice around the lead blob in Metallo's chest compartment. It took only a few moments for her to do what Metallo could not, even with the cutting torch.

Then the hero carefully disconnected all the wires and circuits attached to Metallo's Kryptonite power source. The Kryptonite was still covered in melted lead inside the villain's chest, so Supergirl was safe from its rays. At last the final circuit was cut, and Supergirl breathed a sigh of relief.

"There's only one more thing I have to do," Supergirl said.

The Girl of Steel picked up Metallo and flew out of the power plant. It took her only a few moments to arrive at S.T.A.R. Labs. It was where the armored truck had been taking the box of Kryptonite before Metallo attacked. The director and a group of scientists greeted the hero.

"There was a little trouble with the armored truck," Supergirl said. "But I can still deliver the Kryptonite you wanted for your research."

She handed over Metallo to the scientists.

"It's not exactly in the original lead container," Supergirl said, "but I'm sure you can find a way to get it out."

Metallo

REAL NAME: John Corben

SPECIES: Cyborg

BASE: Metropolis

HEIGHT: 6 feet 5 inches

WEIGHT: 200 pounds

EYES: Green

HAIR: None

POWERS/ABILITIES: Superhuman strength, speed, and durability. He is also unable to feel pain and can release deadly radiation at Kryptonian foes from his Kryptonite power source.

BIOGRAPHY: A hardened criminal, John Corben was once employed by Lex Luthor. The criminal mastermind infected Corben with a deadly virus and then offered to "save" Corben by having him undergo a medical procedure. Upon awakening, Corben felt unimaginably strong. Unfortunately, his brain had been transplanted into a cyborg body, making him a shell of his former self. Unable to feel anything but the cold embrace of metal, Corben has developed an evil side, making him a major threat to all of Metropolis.

- Corben was simply a pawn in Luthor's attempt to create a super-villain capable of defeating Superman. Upon discovering the truth, Metallo swore to destroy Luthor for transforming him into a metallic monster.

- Metallo's heart is made of pure Kryptonite, which powers his exoskeleton. Without the alien mineral, Corben's cyborg body would be completely powerless.

- When the man of metal clashes with Supergirl and Superman, sparks really fly! Metallo is capable of stunning them with his powerful cyborg punches. By opening his chest compartment, Metallo can bathe both Kryptonians in his Kryptonite's lethal radiation.

BIOGRAPHIES

Author

Laurie S. Sutton has been reading comics since she was a kid. She grew up to become an editor for Marvel, DC Comics, Starblaze, and Tekno Comics. She has written Adam Strange for DC, Star Trek: Voyager for Marvel, plus Star Trek: Deep Space Nine and Witch Hunter for Malibu Comics. There are long boxes of comics in her closet where there should be clothing and shoes. Laurie has lived all over the world and currently resides in Florida.

Illustrator

Cartoonist **Gregg Schigiel** is the creator/author/illustrator of the superhero/fairy tale mash-up Pix graphic novels and was a regular contributor to Spongebob Comics. Outside of work, Mr. Schigiel bakes prize-winning cookies, enjoys comedy, and makes sure he drinks plenty of water. Learn more at greggschigiel.com.

GLOSSARY

alloy (AL-oi)—a combination of two or more metals

arc welder (ARK WELD-uhr)—a device that cuts or joins metals using heat generated by an electric arc

compartment (kuhm-PART-muhnt)—a separate space inside an object, often used for keeping something apart from other things

generator (JEN-uh-ray-tur)—a machine that produces electricity by turning a magnet inside a coil of wire

hydroelectric (hye-droh-i-LEK-trik)—to do with the production of electricity from moving water

meteorite (MEE-tee-ur-ite)—a meteoroid that lands on Earth's surface

meteoroid (MEE-tee-ur-oyd)—a rocky or metallic chunk of matter that travels through space

radiation (ray-dee-AY-shuhn)—tiny particles sent out from radioactive material

radioactive (ray-dee-oh-AK-tiv)—having to do with materials that give off potentially harmful invisible rays or particles

stamina (STAM-uh-nuh)—the energy and strength to keep doing something for a long time

DISCUSSION QUESTIONS

1. Why does Metallo want the Kryptonite in the armored truck? What do you think he might do with it?

2. What is Metallo's most useful weapon in his battle against Supergirl? Is it his super-strength, his arm laser, or his Kryptonite power source? Why do you think the one you chose is the strongest?

3. Supergirl tries a lot of different ways to stop Metallo. Most of them fail to slow down the villain. Why do you think she keeps trying instead of just giving up?

WRITING PROMPTS

1. Supergirl uses many of her superpowers to battle Metallo. Which one do you like best? Write a paragraph about why you would like to have that power. Then draw a picture of yourself using it.

2. Imagine that you are a newspaper reporter who witnessed Supergirl's battle with Metallo. Write a news story that describes what you saw from where you were standing.

3. At the end of the story, Supergirl hands Metallo and the Kryptonite over to the scientists at S.T.A.R. Labs. What do you think happens next? Write another chapter that continues Metallo's story.

LOOK FOR MORE

DC SUPER HERO ADVENTURES

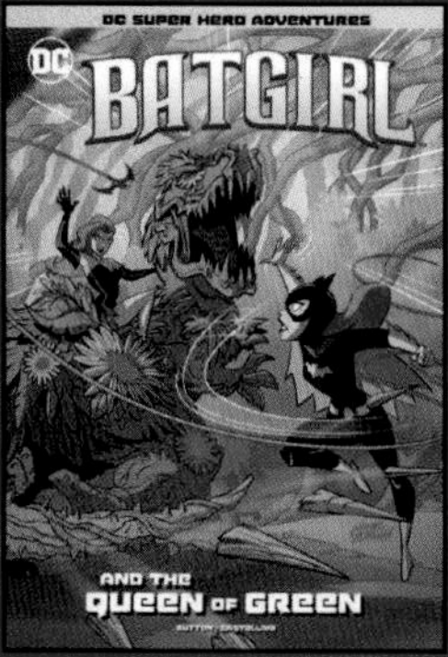
DC SUPER HERO ADVENTURES
BATGIRL
AND THE
QUEEN OF GREEN

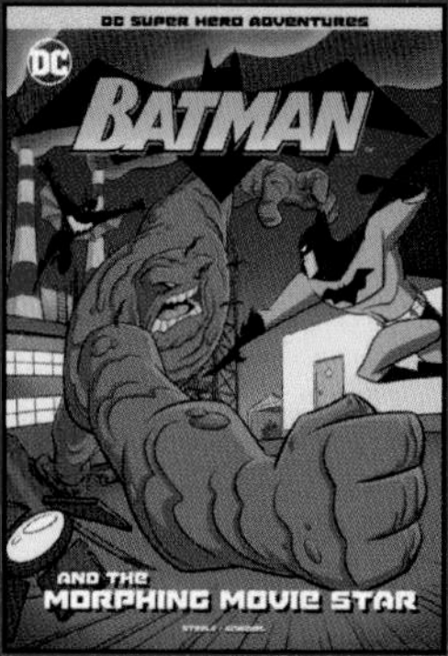
DC SUPER HERO ADVENTURES
BATMAN
AND THE
MORPHING MOVIE STAR

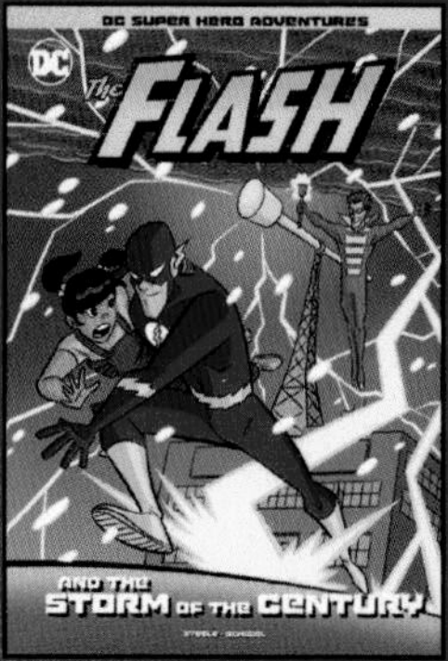
DC SUPER HERO ADVENTURES
The FLASH
AND THE
STORM OF THE CENTURY

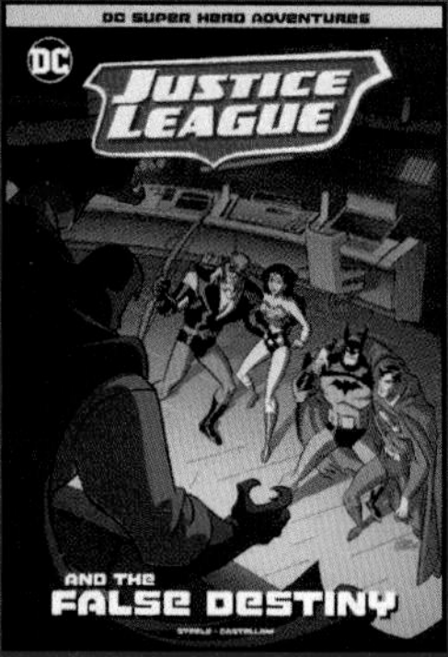
DC SUPER HERO ADVENTURES
JUSTICE LEAGUE
AND THE
FALSE DESTINY

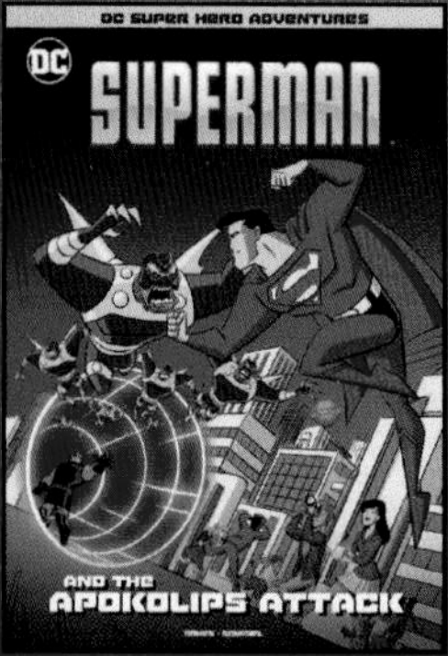
DC SUPER HERO ADVENTURES
SUPERMAN
AND THE
APOKOLIPS ATTACK

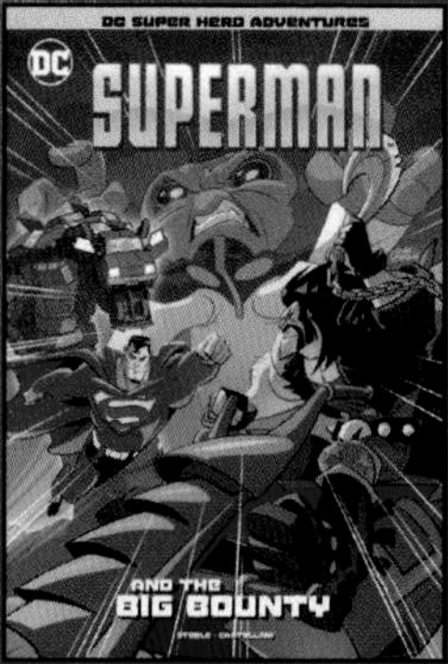
DC SUPER HERO ADVENTURES
SUPERMAN
AND THE
BIG BOUNTY

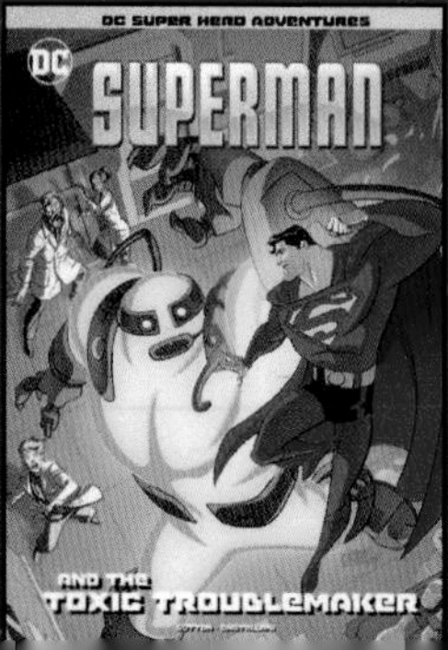
DC SUPER HERO ADVENTURES
SUPERMAN
AND THE
TOXIC TROUBLEMAKER

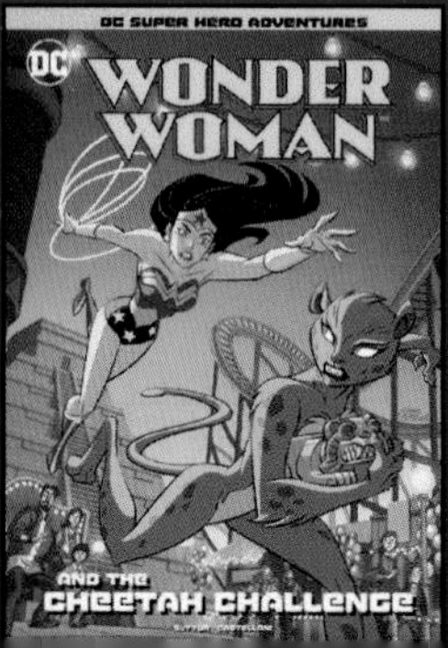
DC SUPER HERO ADVENTURES
WONDER WOMAN
AND THE
CHEETAH CHALLENGE

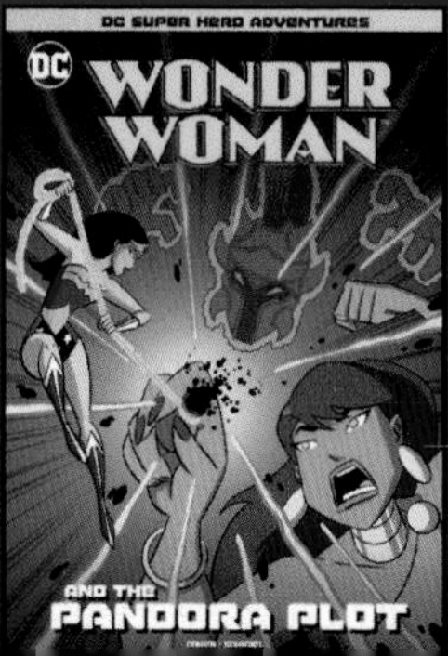
DC SUPER HERO ADVENTURES
WONDER WOMAN
AND THE
PANDORA PLOT